I0583759

LOVE AND ALIENS

LOVE AND ALIENS

DRAGON APPROVED™ BOOK EIGHT

RAMY VANCE

MICHAEL ANDERLE

DISRUPTIVE IMAGINATION

THE LOVE AND ALIENS TEAM

Thanks to the JIT Readers

Kelly O'Donnell
Diane L. Smith
Dorothy Lloyd
Kathleen Fettig
Deb Mader
John Ashmore

If we've missed anyone, please let us know!

Editor
The Skyhunter Editing Team

This Book is a work of fiction. All of the characters, organizations, and events portrayed in this novel are either products of the author's imagination or are used fictitiously. Sometimes both.

Copyright © 2021 by Ramy Vance & Michael Anderle
Cover Art by Jake @ J Caleb Design
http://jcalebdesign.com / jcalebdesign@gmail.com
Cover copyright © LMBPN Publishing
A Michael Anderle Production

LMBPN Publishing supports the right to free expression and the value of copyright. The purpose of copyright is to encourage writers and artists to produce the creative works that enrich our culture.

The distribution of this book without permission is a theft of the author's intellectual property. If you would like permission to use material from the book (other than for review purposes), please contact support@lmbpn.com. Thank you for your support of the author's rights.

LMBPN Publishing
PMB 196, 2540 South Maryland Pkwy
Las Vegas, NV 89109

First US Edition, April 2020
Version 1.01, February 2021
eBook ISBN: 978-1-64202-833-1
Print ISBN: 978-1-64202-834-8

DEDICATION

To Waleed and Rana ... romance is in the air!

—Ramy

To Family, Friends and
Those Who Love
to Read.
May We All Enjoy Grace
to Live the Life We Are
Called.

— Michael

CHAPTER ONE

Myrddin declared a holiday at the Wasp's Nest, the first ever. Most of the staff didn't know what to do with their time, and none of the students did.

Other than Alex Bound.

She knew exactly how she was going to spend her day off. And who she would be spending it with.

The wind was rushing past Alex's face, bringing out the red in her cheeks. She almost gasped for breath. The cold air had come out of nowhere, but it was refreshing. She continued to climb into the clouds as if she were trying to get as far away from the ground as possible.

Her dragon, Chine, had been silent for most of the ride, trying to give Alex space. It was a big day for her, and they'd discussed the proper boundaries the night before.

The reason it was such a big day was that Jim was flying in his mech dragon next to Alex, both of them heading toward some destination Jim had picked out. There were many ways in which Alex could see this day going terribly wrong, and each of them had something to do with her. They were generally vague notions, but if she thought long enough, a crystal-clear version of her screwing things up would manifest itself.

Alex had no idea why she was so nervous. She'd been through much more nerve-wracking experiences over the last few months. She was thousands of feet in the air on the back of an ether dragon, which would have been enough to freak most people out. Going out with Jim should have been a walk in the park. *I wonder if he's taking me to a park?* Alex thought. *We didn't bring anything to eat.*

A gust of wind pushed past Alex and sent another set of shivers down her spine. She tapped the environmental control on her dragon anchor and felt her suit warming up.

Jim had hardly said anything since the two of them had left the Wasp's Nest, the main base of the dragonriders. He had been all jokes and flirty glances when Alex had been getting her dragon ready. Now there was comm silence between the two of them.

Alex wondered if Jim was as nervous as she was. This was *technically* a date. Maybe everyone was nervous on their first dates, but that didn't make any sense for Jim and her. They had spent years playing *Middang3ard* VR together, and since then, they had gone on several death-defying missions as members of the dragonriders corps. She'd think they could hold a simple conversation.

Yet here they were, flying through a perfect sky, on the way to a date they were both looking forward to, riding in complete silence.

What did people do in situations like this? Alex wished she knew what to say, but any time she felt like she was supposed to say something, she froze. It was almost as if awkward silences made her brain shut off.

Was it awkward, though? Wasn't one sign of a good friendship that you could be comfortable being quiet with someone? What if that was all this was—just two friends going out? Jim hadn't said it was a date...or he hadn't used those words specifically. What if this was just one of those "friends" type of things?

Fighting the Dark One's forces was nothing compared to the stress of this ambiguity.

Alex cleared her throat and looked at Jim as she hit her comm. "So, where did you find out about this place?"

Jim looked through his cockpit's windshield as he answered. "Gill told me about it," he replied. "Said it was a nice, romantic place."

Alex felt a dagger in her chest. *Figures I'd say something that would bring up Gill.* She still hadn't thought about her feelings about Gill, but she'd already made up her mind about Jim. It didn't seem like Gill's feelings had been hurt, either. *I mean, he did recommend a romantic place for Jim to take me. He can't be too heartbroken,* Alex thought.

Chine interrupted Alex's rambling train of thought. *You seem to be having a problem speaking to the human you're infatuated with. Perhaps you two could talk about the weather?*

Chine, shut up. I'm not having a hard time talking. Just, this is my first date.

Chine chuckled as he soared higher. *Ah, human mating rituals. Your species is downright adorable when you're trying to—*

Alex interrupted Chine, shouting, "Wait, who said anything about mating? This is just a first date. Like, my first date ever." Alex realized she was speaking out loud and not telepathically directing her thoughts toward Chine.

And her comm was still on.

Jim was looking at Alex, trying to hold back his laughter. "I'm not laughing at the first date thing. I mean, it's my first date too. You knew this was a date, right?"

"Of course, I knew it was a date. I'm not dense. What the hell did you think was so funny?"

Jim pointed at Chine, who was lazily blowing out small

ether fireballs to dispel the clouds in front of him. "Just the whole telepathy thing you have to do with Chine. I'm very happy I don't have to deal with that. Mechs don't talk, and they can't give me shit."

"Haven't you ever heard of the ghost in the machine? Maybe it'll grow its own soul."

Jim opened his cockpit and stretched his arms out, letting the mech fly on autopilot. "I'd prefer not to think about that. These things are already hard enough to handle. I don't even want to think about contending with a real personality."

"Guess that's the difference between us dragonriders and you mech riders. We can interact. I'm pretty sure all you guys are doing are pressing buttons and hoping the thing doesn't break down on you."

Jim feigned taking a shot to the heart and fell back into his mech. "Damn, if that's your idea of flirting, you might want to put on some gloves. You're going to leave my ego way too bruised."

"Dude, I haven't even started teasing you yet. This isn't even the first round." Alex started shadowboxing, tossing jabs and hooks at imaginary foes. "You're lucky you're not in the ring with me," she said as she jabbed. "They call me 'Thunderfists' out on the mean streets."

"Oh, really. Thunderfists? When did they start doing that?"

"First thing my mother said when I was born," Alex said, putting on a fake Southern accent. "Mamma said I punched my way straight out into the world. Been a slugger ever since. What's your story, cowboy?" she asked.

Jim steered his mech closer to Alex's dragon and leaned out of the cockpit. "My story? Oh, I just came in with the wind. I don't have a story," he replied with a horrendous Western accent. "And I'd like to keep it that way. Stories hold you down. Make you all weighty and heavy. Nope, a man like me don't need no story. We just roll with the wind. Can't lose what you don't collect."

Alex giggled as she noticed how widely Jim was smiling at her. It was the kind of smile that made her want to stop what she was doing, whatever it was, and just stare for a little bit. "You're not too bad at that. Wouldn't have pegged you as one for improv."

"Before *Middang3ard* VR, I used to do a *lot* of tabletop role-playing. Sometimes we'd just roll random characters, and you'd have to pretend to be a klepto orc or a skittish elf for a month. Kinda seems funny in hindsight. You know, with having to fight orcs and having a drow for a teammate."

Alex was glad she had never cared much for fantasy books or games. It was much more interesting to be experiencing it all for the first time. The most she had ever learned of fantasy had been from *Middang3ard* VR, but now she was living the real thing. "How much longer until we get to this place?" she asked.

Jim looked at his dashboard while he pushed his upper lip out with his tongue. "Probably another half-hour. I know it's a little far, but it's supposed to be beautiful."

Alex half-wondered why Gill knew about it. He wasn't from this realm, so he must have recently gone there. "I love riding," Alex said. "It could be six hours away, and I'd be glad for the ride."

Jim started to slowly bring his mech into a descent, getting out of the clouds. "You know, I can't remember the last time I had a full day off. Between training and these recent crazy missions, I thought I was going to lose my mind."

Alex agreed. It had been too long without a break. The last few months had been nothing but a blur. Between the invasion of the Dark Nest, fighting a reality-warping meteor and being recruited for a rescue mission in an orcish arena,

Alex had hardly had a chance to catch her breath. And that wasn't counting all the regular classes and training sessions Alex and the rest of Team Boundless had to attend.

Myrddin had informed the Nest that today was going to be a national holiday but hadn't elaborated on whose people or which nations were host to it. Alex thought it was just a way for Myrddin to give the Nest a chance to relax without looking like he'd gone soft. It was a good idea.

Jim kicked his feet up in the cockpit as he pulled out a soda. He whistled for Alex's attention and mimed opening the can, and when Alex nodded, he tossed one over to her. "Wish we would have gotten more than a day off," Alex grumbled. "I feel like my nerves have been fraying for the last week."

Jim nodded his agreement before saying, "Yeah, I'm not sure if they think running us ragged is going to make us tougher or if they don't realize we're tired. I mean, my dad used to talk about how bad boot camp was sometimes. Doubt this is much different. At least we're clear of getting any more missions. I can deal with school and training."

School and training were easier than missions, but Alex didn't want to do either of them. Spending a week flying with Chine and goofing off seemed like a more appropriate reward for saving a realm and thwarting the attack on the Nest. That was probably reserved for heroes, though, and Alex was just a soldier, one of many.

Jim leaned over the edge of his mech's cockpit and peered down. Then he sat back down and closed his cockpit, tilting his mech slightly to the left. "Pixies in trouble," he said through the comm.

Alex chuckled and shook her head. "You've been hanging out too much with Jollies. I don't think I know enough pixie slang to make sense out of that," she replied.

"No, I mean, there are pixies down there. And they look like they might be in trouble."

Alex looked down. She didn't have the benefit of Jim's mech's surveillance tech, but she had something that a lot of other people would have envied: magical dragon eyes. She was still learning how to master them, but every day was easier than the previous one. Focusing on things beyond human capacity was a parlor trick now.

Alex closed her eyes, took a quick breath, and opened them, looking down thousands of feet in perfect clarity. It was a feat that would have given her a migraine for days a few weeks earlier.

Jim was right. There was a group of pixies near the surface who were fleeing from something. Alex looked back a little way and could see that the pixies were trying to avoid a group of giants. "Great," Alex moaned. "Not even a full day off."

"We could just postpone until later. You know where I live."

"You live across the hall from me."

"And yet you never try to sneak in."

Alex blushed, remembering a few nights ago when she had snuck out of her room and stood in front of Jim's room for nearly five minutes, debating whether or not she should knock. She stood there until Gill passed by, smirking a little but remaining silent. "Oh, come on! Pack up the jokes and let's go help those pixies before they get crushed."

CHAPTER TWO

The pixies Alex and Jim were worried about were currently flying through a forest, trying to take advantage of the trees as cover. They were nearly a hundred of them—a small tribe, since woodland pixies tended to keep their tribes smaller. The trees were not doing much to hide the pixies, though, since their anxiety and fear could easily be seen in their glowing, changing pigment.

There was a good amount of distance between the pixies and the giants, but it was being closed fast. Although the pixies were fast, the giants had the benefit of being huge. These giants were larger than any Alex had seen so far. As she'd learned through her studies, there were dozens of different species.

These seemed to be *yhomir* or forest giants. They usually kept to themselves and avoided conflict whenever possible. But as Alex had learned, a creature under the Dark One's sway rarely acted as it should. Creatures and sentient beings would behave in ways contrary to their ideals or traditions. Alex was terrified of what would happen if the Dark One were to ever take control of humanity.

The *yhomir* were closing on the pixies as the seconds ticked by. The giants were now running nearly on all fours, their lanky, muscular arms almost touching the ground as they ran forward, their mouths foaming and eyes red. They looked as if they'd been reduced to some feral pre-giant form, devoid of intelligence or understanding.

The pixies were no longer trying to hide. They were screaming and flying as fast as they could.

Alex and Jim descended into the forest. The trees were a problem Alex hadn't had to deal with yet. Generally, the battles she had fought had taken place in the sky or open spaces, since her enemies usually were riding something as well. Today, that was not the case. The farther the pixies ran into the forest, the thicker the trees became.

The forest was almost dense enough to block out the sun. As Alex got closer to the tree line, she commed Jim and asked, "You got any ideas on how to deal with this one?"

Jim shrugged as he steered away from Alex. "There's no way we can take on all those giants head-on. We need to cull their numbers. Did you count how many of them there were?"

"At least thirty. I don't know why they'd need that many to go after those pixies. You think it's the Dark One? What would he want with a bunch of woodland pixies?"

"What does he ever want? Seems like the guy wants to dominate just for the sake of it. There doesn't seem to be any reason behind this whole war, or none that I can figure out. None that anyone is telling us."

Alex directed her thoughts toward Chine. *Do you think you can maneuver through the trees?*

Chine replied, *I will be able to move more easily on the ground. The trees are too close together for flying, but I won't lose any speed on my feet. It would be a more effective strategy.*

Alex commed Jim again. "Hey, how's your ground game look in that thing?"

Jim flipped a couple of switches and brought up his holo-screen. "Should be good. Faster than a giant. We're supposed to be getting these things upgraded later this week. That nerd-farmer we went on that mission with is supposedly a genius. Convinced Roy to let her take a look at the mechs."

Alex was interested in what the nerd-farmer (Alex knew the kid's name was Abby, but nerd-farmer sounded kind of endearing in her head) had in store for the mechs, but now wasn't the time to talk shop. Those pixies were going to be dust if Alex and Jim didn't move in fast enough. "All right, I say we take a stealth approach. See if we can sneak up behind them and thin the ranks a little," she suggested.

Jim hit a button on his dashboard and his mech faded from sight. "When the hell did you figure out you could do that?" Alex exclaimed.

Jim's head popped back into visibility for a second, just long enough for Alex to see his smug smile. "Got a new batch of augments earlier today. Didn't think I'd get a chance to try this one out, but now seems like the perfect chance."

The two descended until they were nearly brushing the trees. Alex relaxed and let her eyes do their work. Because her eyes were modeled after Chine's, Alex had all of the benefits of a dragon's vision. She could see the heat signatures of the giants beneath her.

After determining their location, she swooped behind them from above and then lowered herself and Chine into the forest.

Chine touched down as lightly as possible, hardly making any noise, and they began to sneak closer to the giants. Chine took the lead on this one because Alex wasn't used to riding her dragon on the ground.

The psychic link between Chine and Alex was strong, and

Alex rarely had to communicate about things like that. It made working together a lot easier.

Alex rarely realized how lizard-like Chine could be, but she was reminded as the dragon slipped in and out of the shadows. His footsteps didn't make a sound.

Jim was out of sight, and Alex hoped he had touched down already as well. She was going to comm him but thought better of it. Giants rarely used tech (something that didn't seem to be affected by the Dark One's influence), but there was always a chance they had some way of detecting electronic communications. Alex had recently been reading about the psychic capabilities of some types of giants. It would be best to play this safe.

For now, Alex would just assume Jim was as competent a rider on the ground as she knew he was in the air. Part of her wished Gill was here instead of Jim for this mission, and it made her feel like crap. Gill was great at stealth, and it would have put some of her worries to rest. Plus, she kind of missed the drow. *Not thinking about that right now,* Alex reminded herself. *Teenage Hormone Hour is scheduled for later.*

Up ahead, Alex could see a giant who was lagging behind the rest of the group. Perfect. Waves of Chine's emotions rolled over Alex. It was something that had just recently started happening. Alex hadn't spoken with the dragon about it yet, but whenever Chine felt something strongly, it would wash over Alex like a fine mist.

So far, it had not been anything complex—mostly boredom and excitement, but this time, it was different. There was something going on within Chine that was almost overpowering. Giddiness was the only way Alex could describe it. It wasn't hard to figure out why, either. Sometimes Alex had an inkling of what was sparking his emotions, but this time, it hit Alex like a slap in the face.

The hunt. Something about hunting the giants was

making Chine as happy as a child with a new toy. Alex thought it was kind of cute, and she let herself get caught up in it as the two of them raced after the lagging giant. Giants weren't known for being forgiving when traveling. If you couldn't keep up, you couldn't keep up. It was a mindset Alex was willing to exploit.

Chine's head snapped forward and he snatched the giant, crushing the huge creature between his jaws. Both Chine and Alex felt extremely satisfied with the sounds of the cracking bones.

Alex hadn't been aware Chine was so good at stealth. All of the battles the two of them had been in so far had been heart-pounding, explosive situations. Alex had never heard of dragons being sneaky, but at the moment, Chine reminded Alex more of a dangerous viper than anything else.

Even with that, it was only a matter of time before the giants realized they were being picked off. Giants weren't dumb, and the darkness of the forest was only going to obscure Alex and Chine for so long. If there had been more riders, Alex could have easily overtaken the giants she was stalking. But she and Jim weren't going to be enough. This was going to turn into a full-on battle eventually.

There was still a fair amount of distance between the main group of giants and the few who had fallen behind. Alex didn't know how many giants Jim had managed to take out, but she knew that once the fight started, they'd still be dealing with the bulk of the giants.

There was a bright flash of heat, something Alex was certain only she and Chine noticed. That must have been Jim. Alex realized that if she focused, she could pick up on Jim's heat signature. She concentrated on finding different levels of heat at the same time.

Jim's mech was hot and blew out her vision. It was

snaking its way, slower but still persistently, through the forest, occasionally stopping to snipe one of the giants.

At the sound of Jim's approach, two of the giants turned, spotting Alex and Chine. They shouted, calling to the other giants, who immediately forgot the pixies they'd been chasing.

One of the giants reached over and ripped a tree up by its roots. The yhomir threw the tree at Chine, who leaped to the side. The tree hit another, exploding into a thousand chunks. That giant really had an arm on him. Alex figured keeping her distance was the best idea. If one of them got hold of Chine, it would be bad news.

The dragon growled as he backed away from the giants. *He must have been thinking the same thing,* Alex thought as she scanned the environment. There wasn't much space to move around with the trees being so densely packed. It was going to be impossible to accurately use Chine's flames without torching the trees.

That would be disastrous. There were a host of creatures and races that lived in the woods. Alex was pretty sure the pixies were residents of the very forest cradling them now. It would mean a lot of deaths and a lot of displacement. There had to be another option.

One of the giants went flying to the left, crumbling under an invisible attack from Jim. The rest of the giants whirled, trying to find the source of the attack. Maybe that was the best approach for the time being: let Jim take out giants from stealth mode, and Alex could clean up the rest of them.

A giant ripped another tree up and swung it like a bat. There was the sound of metal cracking, and sparks flew as Jim became visible.

Jim's mech tumbled back, nearly toppling over. He obviously hadn't been expecting to be found out so soon. "Damn it," he muttered into the comm. "Any ideas on how we're going to take care of this?"

There was no time to form a plan. Instead, Alex trusted her gut, and right now, her gut was telling her to engage. Fight. "We get in close," Alex cried out. "Hit hard and aggressively."

"I'm starting to think that's your solution for everything."

"You're welcome to solve this problem however you want. I know what I'm doing."

Alex pulled back on her dragon anchor, sending Chine leaping at the closest giant.

The giant saw Chine coming and braced itself for the attack. As Chine snapped his jaws closed, the giant grabbed the side of Chine's mouth, keeping the dragon from closing his jaws.

Alex could see that this was going to be a fight. The other giants were starting to surround her. She stretched out her hand to call her scythe blade from her dragon anchor, and it materialized in her right hand. She twirled it elegantly, relishing in the sound of the gears whirring in her robotic arm.

Even though it had taken some time to get used to it, Alex preferred using her robotic arm for fighting. She had a much broader range of motion and more strength than she'd had before.

She wasn't going to leave her dragon to deal with the giant by himself. She unhooked herself from the anchor and ran up the length of Chine's back to his head, then slashed the giant's throat, severing its head.

Its body fell, and the rest of the giants' eyes flashed as if they realized that they were no longer the only predators. Alex and Chine were their equals, if not more. *Guess I'll just have to prove it to you, asshats,* Alex thought to herself.

Chine whipped around, slashing the giant behind him

with his tail as his rider ran down his right wing, slashing at the giants who were attempting to crowd him.

At Alex's side, Jim was firing his machine gun, cutting down the ones who were too stupid to turn away from the bullets.

Suddenly, as if they had all received a command, the giants dropped to the ground, hunching so their arms scraped the forest floor. Then they sprang into the air, grabbing the branches of the trees and swinging up into the dark canopy like huge monkeys.

Jim and Alex looked around the clearing. All of the giants were gone. "Uh, what just happened?" Alex asked.

"I don't know, but giants aren't supposed to move like that. Last time I saw one, they were not that agile. I thought that was kinda their thing, you know? Big and slow."

"Explains how they were able to keep up with the pixies."

A heavy kick hit Alex in the side, throwing her off of Chine. She hit a tree hard and gasped for breath. "Shit," she muttered as she stood up. She looked above her. Giants were hanging from tree branches, their red eyes glaring.

Alex groaned as she stood up. *All right, I didn't want to go the whole-hog, but we might as well.* She ran back to the dragon. *Let's tear through these guys, Chine!*

Chine didn't need to be told twice. The dragon roared, letting everything in the forest know of his presence. Then he leaped into the trees while Jim watched, amazed at Alex's brazenness.

Alex cut through a giant while Chine snorted a small, controlled stream of fire, burning the branches out from under a couple of giants. Jim saw his opening and bolted toward the creatures, his machine guns blazing, cutting them down as soon as they hit the ground.

Above, Alex and the dragon were making short work of the giants. They moved in unison, Alex traversing Chine's body as if he were a canvas for her to paint on. They annihilated the giants that remained almost before the monsters knew it.

Chine landed on the ground as Jim wandered over. "You know, if you want, next time I could just stand on the sidelines. I have no problem with you taking care of everything," Jim joked.

Alex looked around at the bodies that littered the forest floor. "Psh, what are you talking about?"

"You and Chine wrecked those giants. I thought they were going to give us a much harder time."

"Eh, they made the mistake of assuming Chine and I were attached at the hip. That, and this big guy seems to be as comfortable in a forest as in the air. Plus, they were interrupting our date. So, how about we go see how those pixies are and get back to it?"

Jim smiled as he opened his cockpit. "Oh, so you're enjoying the romancing?"

Alex started toward where she thought the pixies would be. "I don't *not* like it."

CHAPTER THREE

Alex and Jim found the pixies huddled in an old mushroom-covered tree log. They were sitting quietly, two of the older ones perched near the opening as lookouts. When they saw two humans approaching, they whistled loudly for the rest of the pixies to come and meet their saviors.

The pixies were ecstatic. They had seen the fight or at least the two sentries had, and told the rest of the pixies what they'd seen. The sentries recognized Jim and Alex as dragonriders. They had heard tales of the riders' prowess in battle and were glad to see that the stories were not exaggerations.

Alex tried not to let the praise go to her head. She was happy they were safe—that was the important thing. But it never hurt to hear nice things. For the most part, being a dragonrider was a thankless job. The corps gave credit when it was due, but it was a circular thing. The people Alex was working to protect had no idea about the kind of work she did.

It was nice to be able to see the joy in the faces of the

pixies. Alex knew she had made a difference. (Not that she thought she hadn't before.) Seeing the pixies safe and well was different, though. It wasn't an abstract concept like the Dark One was. This was tangible. And sometimes that was all Alex needed—just be able to hold on to something, to know it was real.

One of the sentries flew up to Alex's face, smiling and glowing bright yellow. "What brought you into the forest anyway?" the pixie asked. "Humans don't usually come out this way, even if the Wasp's Nest is so close. We hardly ever see humans."

Alex figured that made sense. "That's because there aren't many other humans around the Nest," Alex said. "Have you met any of the other dragonriders?"

"Oh, yes, many. There are a few elves who come to our woods, and pixies. Also, a young drow...he is the quietest of all. Sometimes we don't even know he's among the trees."

Jim laughed as he shook his head. "That would be Gill," he said mostly to himself. "Only quiet person I know who's able to make that kind of impression."

The sentry flew closer to Alex's face. "You still haven't told me what brought you to the forest."

"Oh, yeah. Well, we were trying to get someplace," Alex said. "But I'm not sure where it was we're going. It was supposed to be a surprise."

The sentries looked at each other, confused by how awkward the two humans were being. "What are you doing in the forest?" one of the sentries inquired.

Jim bashfully scratched the back of his head. "Uh, well, we're on a date."

The sentry still seemed to be in the dark. "What is 'a date?'"

Jim's face went red as he cleared his throat. "Guess it's like a pre-mating ritual. I mean, kinda like an equivalent for pixies." He turned to Alex, throwing his hands up. "Not saying that's what I'm trying to do or anything. It's just that pixies don't do dates, but they have those rituals."

Alex couldn't bring herself to meet Jim's eyes, and he turned back and started talking to the pixie sentries, who had flown closer to speak more quietly. When the sentries finally gave Jim his space, he was shaking his head and blushing slightly. "They want to escort us on our date," he explained. "As a thank you."

"Why would we want a pixie escort? This isn't my high school prom."

"Alex, you were homeschooled. You didn't have a prom."

Alex shrugged off Jim's critique of her wit. "Doesn't matter. You get the point I'm making," she retorted.

Jim came over to Alex and smiled that smile that had recently started to make her stomach flutter. "Trust me, it's totally gonna be worth it. Sun's about to set and everything. It's a great idea."

"All right. As long as this doesn't turn out to be anything weird."

The sun had set, and darkness had settled over the valley. The moon hung crooked and swollen like a giant white eye peering at that which could not be known. Alex had always loved full moons, but although tonight's was gorgeous, it was nothing compared to what she was a part of.

The pixies were glowing as bright as they could, surrounding Alex and Jim as they made their way through the forest and down to a meadow of wildflowers. Those were glowing as well, although in muted tones.

The parade of lights continued through the meadow, past the flowers and up into the hills. Alex couldn't take her eyes off of the pixies, who were also singing quietly, a low and solemn tune that added an air of gravity to their short journey. Alex would not have connected it with pixies. Gone was their lightheartedness; instead, there was a weight in the song that hung as heavy as heartbreak.

It was a sobering experience, almost like a meditation. Jim was right; it was a great idea.

As they traveled under the moonlight with the song of the pixies filling the air, they descended into the valley. At the bottom was a pond roughly thirty feet across, surrounded by an outcropping of trees. There was sand around the lake, and even from far away, it looked soft. Steam was rising from the water. "You brought your bathing suit, right?" Jim asked.

Alex had thought Jim was joking about swimming. It had been freezing the last few nights, but she had worn it under her armor just to be safe. Even though Jim joked a lot, he rarely advised doing something unless it was important.

The pixies continued down the hill with Alex and Jim until they stood before the lake. Alex dismounted from Chine, and Jim exited his mech. They stood on the shore of the lake, watching the steam rise. "How hot is it?" Alex asked.

"Gill said it's about ninety degrees on a night like this. He thought it was weird we were bringing bathing suits. Apparently, drow skinny-dip."

Alex put all her mental effort into not letting her imagination run wild with that idea. Instead, she hit her dragon anchor, and her armor slid up into her anchor. Jim did the same, and they both walked over to the lake. Alex dipped her toe into the water. Gill hadn't lied. The lake was practically the temperature of a hot tub.

Slowly Alex lowered herself into the water, the heat shooting up her legs as if it were fire. At first, it was too hot, but the water instantly became relaxing. She oozed into the pool as if she'd become water.

Jim wasn't too far behind her. He took a little more time to get his legs wet, but once he was knee-deep, he waded farther into the lake.

The two swam slowly around each other, circling in silence. The moon shone down on them as if in agreement with what it beheld.

Alex couldn't remember the last time she'd gone swimming. This was the first time since she'd been magically given her sight. She thought about mentioning it to Jim but decided not to. Sometimes it felt better not to be constantly mentioning how awesome her first experiences were.

But she took it all in: the reflection of the moon against the water, Jim's bare chest glistening with small beads of water, the constantly shifting colors of the pixies who were dancing above them like streaking stars that had come down to join them.

Alex and Jim didn't speak much. They swam instead. When they were not swimming, they went back to the bank of the lake and lay down on the soft sand as the warm waters washed over their bodies. When they did speak, it was of nothing in particular. Stories told in snippets. The occasional laugh or giggle.

Time stopped for a bit.

Finally, after a long period of silence, while lying on the bank of the pond, Alex sighed and said, "I think I really needed this."

Jim was waving his hand back and forth in the water. He looked up absentmindedly, as if the heat from the lake had drained him of his thoughts. "I think we both did."

Alex stared up at the moon. Everything felt perfect. She couldn't imagine it could be better. "I'm glad you asked me," she said. "It'll be nice to come back here with everyone. But I'm glad that it's just us this time."

As Alex stared up the sky, something bright and green streaked across. It looked like someone had carved open the sky and whatever was underneath had bled green. It was gone within a moment, only a flash. And that was all the attention Alex gave the streak.

CHAPTER FOUR

Alex and Jim had lost track of time. It was a pleasant feeling, one Alex couldn't really recall having shared with another person before. Especially not such interesting conversation. Jim didn't seem to like small talk very much. He kept asking Alex questions that made her stop and think.

That wasn't to say Alex wasn't trying to do the same thing. This was the first time they'd gotten to talk for an extended period of time outside of VR or work. It felt like they had a lot of catching up to do. Or at least, to get to know each other.

As Jim told Alex about the first time he'd ever broken a bone, she noticed that the streak was still bright in the sky, almost as if it had slowed its descent. When Jim was finished speaking, Alex pointed at it. "Seems like that's been there for a while, right?" she asked.

Jim smiled as he leaned back to look at the green streak. "Was my story that boring?"

"Are you going to give me crap about looking up at the sky when it's so beautiful tonight?"

"When you put it like that, I'll pull my foot out of my

mouth. And to answer your question, yeah. It does seem odd that it's been like that for so long."

Alex stood, walked over to Chine, and grabbed her HUD. She stared through the visor at the streak. "I'm going to check in with HQ about this," she said before hitting her comm. "Hey, I'd like you to check out my coordinates. I'm seeing an anomaly in the sky. Not quite sure about it. I was just wondering if you could take a look at it or watch it."

An obnoxiously gruff voice came over the comm. "What are you doing out that far? That's a restricted area," the voice chastised.

"No, it's not," Alex replied. "There aren't any restricted areas around the Nest."

"Oh, well, it's not for first-year students. That's what I mean by 'restricted.'"

It was obvious to Alex that whoever was talking to her was messing around. "Okay, I'm not in the mood to play games right now," Alex said, certain that whoever was on the comm was someone she knew. "Who is this?"

The gruff voice disappeared and was replaced by the bright, cheery tones of Jollies, a pixie, one of the other members of Team Boundless. "Aw, you suck the fun out of everything," she whined.

"Only when I'm trying to seriously ask something. What are you doing on watch tonight?" Alex asked.

Jollies sighed as she explained. "Well, first-year students get the short end when it comes to night shifts. Brath and me got them two days in a row. Say hi, Brath."

Brath's annoyed voice came through the comm. "I don't know why I have to say hi," the gnome groaned. "It's not like she called *me*."

"She didn't call me either, jerk. She called the night watch, and seeing as how you are also working the night watch, the call applies to you too. Now say hello."

Brath grumbled under his breath before he said, "Hello. How's the date going?"

Alex felt her face flush with a mixture of embarrassment and irritation. She had figured Jollies was going to give her a hard time about it, but she would have thought it would be beneath Brath. Although, Brath *was* Gill's best friend. It wouldn't be out of the question to assume Brath was being defensive, but Gill hadn't seemed the least bit bothered by Alex and Jim going on a date.

Jollies erupted into gales of giggles at Brath's question. "Oh, my goodness, I completely forgot you two were on a date right now. Are you guys holding hands? Did he kiss you yet? Does he smell good, like cologne-good, or did he just decide to go the human 'this is how I smell' route? You should have tried the pixie perfume I told you about, the one my mom sent me. It's soooo good, and I think you would have loved it. But I need details—"

Alex interrupted Jollies. "I'm still on the date. Like, Jim's right here next to me."

"Oh. Kinda awkward to be talking on the comm while you're on a date."

Jim's voice came on. "Just so you all know, the comm is an open channel. I can hear you."

Alex wished she could shrivel up and fade from the realm.

Jim spoke again. "Whatever we are doing is our business, though, Jollies. Maybe you should ask Alex when the entire Nest doesn't have the ability to hear you."

Alex could imagine Jollies pouting. If there was one thing the pixie hated, it was having her fun taken away from her. She would probably be upset about this for the next couple of days. Even if Alex told her roommate what happened in explicit detail, it wouldn't be enough. She wouldn't be satisfied.

"Fine," Jollies finally said. "I'll talk to you in private about it when you get back, Alex. But I'm going to want all the details. Even things you don't want to admit to yourself."

"Sheesh, Jollies, you make it sound horrifying."

Alex could practically see Jollies turning a different color as she spoke, jumping from red to black and maybe deep purple. "*All* the details," the pixie growled. Then her voice returned to its chipper tones. "So, what was it you wanted to talk to us about?"

Alex had almost forgotten the reason she had called the night watch. "There's a weird light in the sky near Jim and me," she explained. "I didn't think anything of it at first, but I don't know, it doesn't look right. It reminds me of the meteor we just recently fought."

Jollies was all business now. Alex wondered how long the pixie had been helping with the night watch. "Oh, then that would be something to pay attention to," Jollies said as professionally as she could be. "It's a good thing you two were out that way. Nothing is showing up on our screens."

"Yeah, I thought it was really weird-looking. So, what now? Will you guys stay up all night watching it?"

"You know, that's exactly what we're going to end up doing. Night watch is *so* boring. Even if there isn't anything important about the light, there's nothing else to do. Brath is refusing to talk to me. Jim gave him some sort of human video game, and he hasn't put it down, even though he's supposed to be helping me with my dragon anatomy quiz."

There was some scuffling over the comm, and Brath yelped in either fear or irritation. "Hey, what the hell do you think you're doing with that?" the gnome shouted. "I swear, if anything happens to it, Jim is going to kill me. And I'll help you with your damn quiz. We're going to be here all night. Don't see what the huge rush is."

Finally, the commotion settled down. Alex had enjoyed the brief chat, but she was much more interested in hanging out with Jim than listening to Jollies and Brath argue. Before Alex could disconnect, she heard Brath asking her to hold on. "Looks like we got a problem," Brath said. "That's not a meteor. That's a ship, and it's still coming down."

Alex sighed, remembering the meteor she'd come across. It had been a living ship that had warped reality around itself. If this was anything like that, it was going to take the whole Nest to deal with it. The last one had almost killed most of Boundless and had resulted in Alex losing her arm. This was the least ideal way a date could have ended up.

Jim was already on his feet, climbing into his mech. Guess that was the end of the date.

Alex had hoped Jim would be happy leaving this for someone else to take care of, but she and Jim were the closest. It made sense for them to check it out. Still, Alex had been hoping to at least get kissed before risking her life again.

CHAPTER FIVE

Alex and Jim thanked the pixies, bade them goodbye, and made their way toward where they expected the ship to come down. It was difficult to tell the trajectory from where they were. Alex wondered if the ship had the same kind of reality-warping abilities as the meteor they'd come across before since both shared the same green streak.

From where Alex was, she figured it could take up to two hours to get to the meteor if it was descending. She logged this information back to the Nest, hoping someone would know what to do with the intel. Being out all night on a mission was the last thing the rider wanted.

Usually, Alex would have jumped at the chance to investigate something like this. She'd always been about the mission, regardless of what it was. Something had been different recently, though, if only just the last few days. Getting up and going to class was a drag. Even running through combat scenarios had been more lackluster than usual.

The only thing she'd been looking forward to in a while

was having some alone time with Jim. Now it looked like that time would be spoiled.

"Chine, what do you make of that thing up ahead?" Alex asked aloud.

Chine snorted loudly as he turned his head to look at the streak of green light. *Here I was thinking you had forgotten about me*, the dragon said, chuckling. *I didn't realize humans were so one-track-minded when they fell in love."*

Alex switched over to her purely mental channel with him and snapped, *Don't tell me you're jumping on board with the immaturity. I would have thought this was above your dragon stateliness.*

There's nothing in my code of honor or action that dictates that I can't have fun or make jokes. Not that you have to worry about it happening often. I like a little teasing, Dustling. As for the streak, I am uncertain. From here, I cannot tell what it is, but it does not fill me with the dread I felt from the rock that we saw before. Whatever this is, I assume it is more benign.

Alex liked the sound of that. It would be nice for something enjoyable to fall from the sky for once. But it wasn't in her nature to be too positive. *Maybe we just aren't close enough to see how bad it is,* she muttered to herself.

As she, Chine, and Jim gained on the object, Alex could tell reality around her hadn't changed, the closer she'd gotten to the green streak. That meant whatever was keeping the object from falling was natural, which somewhat put Alex at ease. "Hey, Night Watch, did you guys get the coordinates we sent you?" she asked.

Jollies' voice crackled over the comm. "Why don't you just use our names?" she asked. "We're the only ones working here. Tonight, at least. And yeah, we did. I uploaded it into the system, and we've been waiting to see if anyone can head over to give you backup. There aren't a whole lot of agents available, though. We're having a hard time getting hold of anyone."

"Where is everyone?"

"Holiday, remember? Most of the Nest is on leave. The only people left are the first-years, and I don't think any first years are up to something this big. Seems like anytime we get involved with something, it gets a lot more intense than most of the first-years can handle. Hell, some of them are still dealing with the attack on the Nest."

Alex had done her share of work to keep from thinking about the attack on the Nest. Much like her lost arm, it was better not to dwell on it. Thinking too much opened a well of emotions Alex didn't want to feel. Painful guilt clenched her chest and bent her thoughts toward that simple feeling of shame she couldn't hide from.

If there was one thing Alex wanted to stop feeling, it was guilt. No matter how she looked at the situation at the Nest, it rubbed the inside of her chest raw. But she could push it away for now. She'd grown pretty good at doing that.

Jollies was still talking, but Alex had zoned out for a second. She brought herself back to the conversation. The pixie was going on about who to send out into the field. "We might be able to pull in some of Roy's mech riders. I don't think those guys ever take a day off, or maybe they don't take their days *on* seriously. Oh, and Gill is going to head over shortly."

It was the first time all day Alex had been happy to hear Gill's name. Having her team around right now sounded like the best idea. "You should avoid confronting the ship, though," Jollies said. "At least until you have a better idea of what you're up against. Otherwise, it could be dangerous."

Alex agreed with the pixie. Getting close and taking a good, long look at whatever the hell had fallen out of the sky sounded like the best idea. "What's Gill's ETA?"

"Probably half an hour or so. He wasn't at the Nest, and he wasn't too far from you guys."

Jim's voice came over the comm. "Wonder what he was up to today?" Jim wondered.

Alex did, as well. Neither she nor Jim was suspicious of Gill like the rest of the cadets at the Nest. Apparently, drow didn't have a good reputation with the other races in the realm. Even though Gill had been a part of several decisive victories, many of the elves at the Nest still looked at him with mistrust.

Alex and Jim were finally close enough to the descending ship to be able to scan it. Alex pulled up her HUD visor and gave the ship a simple yet thorough scan. She didn't bother looking at the information but sent it straight to the Nest.

What Alex really cared about couldn't be seen through the visor. She squinted, activating her superb dragon vision and focusing on the energy trail around the ship. It was definitely the same energy that had been attached to the meteor Team Boundless had fought. That meant that even if this wasn't the same kind of ship that had come through before, it had come from the same place.

In addition to the energy, Alex could see there was a host of vrosks and harpies near the ship. *Great,* Alex thought. *Had to bring friends along with you.* Alex was preparing to report to the Nest that the ship was definitely going to be a problem. Then she looked closer.

The creatures surrounding the ship were attacking it, both the vrosks and the harpies biting at the ship's steel sides. *Now that's interesting,* Alex thought to herself. She commed Jollies. "Hey, so there's a shit-ton of dark creatures around the ship, but they're going after it. I think this might be something the Dark One wants."

Jollies answered quickly. "If that's the case, you need to stay a good distance away. You two just keep an eye on things until Gill gets there. We don't want to escalate anything beyond what we're staffed for at the moment."

That made sense. Alex was about to disconnect when a voice broke over her comm as her HUD flashed the message **Urgent**.

Alex picked up. Myrddin, the ancient wizard responsible for the majority of humanity's resistance against the Dark One, spoke up, and he sounded drunk off his ass. "Alex!" he bellowed.

Alex was glad her comm was partially mental and not completely physical because the volume of Myrddin's voice would have ruptured her eardrum. She could practically smell the booze through the comm. "Yes, sir?"

"Just got your message from the Nest. A bit of a problem…yes, bit of a problem. Most of the staff at the Nest is gone. Vacation. You know all about that. But…but…what were we talking about again?"

"I think you called concerning the ship, sir?"

"Ah, yes…yes…well, you see, that ship is going to be a problem. We can't just have other-dimensional ships landing anytime they want to, but I'm going to need you to wait for backup. Just wait—"

Alex was trying to be polite, but she felt like Myrddin was wasting her time. "Sir, Jollies just told me not to engage. What's your position on that, sir?" A loud cheer bellowed through the comm. "Where are you, sir?"

Myrddin burped loudly before shouting something unintelligible at someone who must have been walking by. "Huge victory on the Dwarf homeworld. Was celebrating, but doesn't seem like the best time. I'm using magic to sober up. Still takes a moment. Be there once I am. An hour, two at the most. Until then, you're in control of the mission. There's a tactical planner on your dragon anchor. It'll give you access to some things you might need. Be in touch in a bit."

Myrddin signed off, and Alex signaled to Jim to stop. He popped open his cockpit and leaned out. "What's going on?"

Alex sat down on Chine and watched the ship in the distance. "Just got off the comm with Myrddin. We're gonna take this mission. Let's find a place to set down, wait for Gill, and figure out what we're going to do."

Jim pointed to a small copse of trees in the distance that seemed to have enough cover to obscure the mech and the dragon. "How about there?"

Alex scanned the area around for the next couple of miles. Those trees would be a good place to start, but they were going to have to keep moving if they were going to catch up with the ship. "Yeah, this'll work. We better get started."

CHAPTER SIX

Alex and Jim touched down and started to make their way through the forest. Alex wanted to find a place where they were not visible to whatever was following the ship, but they could still get enough intel to make sure they weren't leading reinforcements into a trap.

Even if all the battle prep classes Alex had been taking were extremely boring, she was glad some of it had rubbed off on her. She'd started to look at fights as something more complicated than "Make a good plan and hope it all works out."

After the last mission Team Boundless had been on, Alex had been able to speak briefly to the leader of another squad who was a few years older than her. Suzuki of the Mundanes had been lauded as one of the best strategists Middang3ard had to offer, and despite his age, some of his battle strategies had been taught in class.

One of the things Suzuki had told her was each battle was shaped by a variety of factors that were determined before the fight took place. Some of those factors were understood on an unconscious level, like size, strength, and things that could be easily seen.

Other factors had to be searched out, and those were often the ones that determined victory or defeat.

Alex had wished she could have spent more time with the Mundanes. It had been refreshing to see so many humans close to her age. Since she had never gone to high school, Alex had only had the experience of cliques at the Nest to learn how people her age acted. Spending time with the Mundanes might have been a relief.

A focused mind was what Alex needed at the moment, but she couldn't seem to keep her thoughts from wandering. Resentment was something she felt strongly. Her mind kept going back to the first few weeks of classes and how most of the first years had completely ignored her. She was angrier at them than she was at Brath, who she'd forgiven. At least Brath'd had the nerve to get in her face.

Her resentment felt like a betrayal, even if she never expressed it. She'd sworn to protect the Nest and all of the people within it. Part of Alex hated them, and she wished she didn't. She wouldn't have wanted anything to happen to any of them, but she despised the way they had cheered for her when she'd given her speech after her first battle. How they'd told her she was so brave for continuing after her arm had been blown off, as if they'd all forgotten how much she struggled, being the first and only human dragonrider. Alex's mother had told her resentment could sneak in and eat at you from the inside, a cancer that would kill you before you realized it. Alex was aware of her feelings, and she did feel like they were killing her.

Jim's voice brought her out from her circular, intrusive thoughts. "Hey, are you okay? You seem kinda spaced out?" he asked.

Alex didn't want to talk to Jim about any of the things she was thinking. He'd either think she was being an ass or was just generally ungrateful. Well, to be honest, there was no way to be certain how Jim would react to her thoughts, but Alex didn't want to risk him being another person who gave her odd looks. "Nothing, just trying to figure out the next move," she said. "Come on."

She pointed to a raised spot in the forest. "We'll be able to get a better view from up here."

The two humans and the dragon made their way up the steady slope until they came to the top. Alex was right, there was a much better view of the ship. From here, it was easier to see the swerving streak the ship had left behind in the sky.

The ship was definitely coming down, but it must still have power because its descent was measured, as if the pilot were trying to conserve as much energy as possible. That would also explain why the ship hadn't bothered fighting off the dark creatures that had attached themselves to it.

At the rate the ship was descending, it could be another two or three hours before it touched the ground. And there was no way to intercept it, given the lack of resources the Nest had at the moment. On a properly staffed day, Alex could have called for a dropship to scoop up the craft. There would have been reinforcements to deal with the dark creatures.

Great day for a holiday, Alex thought.

Jim exited from his mech and walked over to the edge, gazing through a pair of binoculars at the scene. Past the forest, the land stretched out, with hills breaking up the flat land. "That doesn't look good," Jim muttered, passing the binoculars to Alex, who waved them away. Instead, she focused.

In the darkness, there were other creatures moving about. Dozens of wargs and giants moved through the shadows toward where they assumed the ship was going to come down. There were more than Alex and Jim could deal with alone—enough to pose a risk if they were to screw up.

These were the visible elements Suzuki had talked to Alex about—the things that would determine if she was going to end up dead. Now was the time to look for those invisible factors.

Alex remembered that Myrddin had told her to check out the tactical planner in her dragon anchor. She hadn't heard anything about it before Myrddin had brought it up, so it was probably a new addition, either from an upgrade or her steady increase in rank.

As Alex pulled up the tactical planner, she noticed Chine was moving uncomfortably. The dragon was probably getting annoyed with his augments. It would be a good idea to take care of that before a fight if there was going to be one. *Hey, Chine, ready to get drained?*

He rolled his shoulders and breathed a small wisp of fire. *I don't think it's necessary at the moment. It is only a slight discomfort.*

Oh, come on. Better safe than sorry, right? It'll only take a little time.

Chine's body relaxed, and he let himself sink onto the soft grass. Alex knew she wasn't going to have to ask again.

Alex walked around to his front legs. She found the dragon anchor insertion slot and slid her hand all the way down the anchor and into it. The anchor covered her skin, which would have been burnt otherwise.

The augments dragons wore for battle were extremely effective, but they had one very bad downside. They were hell on a dragon's body, constantly tearing the flesh and burning them by drawing so much of the dragon's fiery, acidic blood. With careful maintenance and communication between rider and dragon, this could be avoided.

That was where the dragon anchors came into use. Not only did the anchors literally anchor the rider to the dragon's back during flight, but they were also used to drain the dragon's augments of draconic fluid and process that fluid through the rider's bloodstream. Once a rider was bound, they became more dragon each day.

The process had never been fully explained to Alex and seemed to be taken for granted by all the other riders and teachers. Alex hadn't gotten over her fear of being seen as an idiot for asking, so the whole situation still was shrouded in mystery. But at the same time, Alex's eyes had the capabilities of a dragon's. She was already more dragon than any of the other cadets.

Alex soaked the draconic fluid into her dragon anchor and let the anchor integrate it into her blood. When she was finished with all the augments, Alex climbed atop Chine and plunged her anchor into the final spot, his spinal augment. That augment was never removed. It was what anchored Alex to the dragon and the dragon to her.

Once the fluid had all been drained, Alex sat down and let the fluid integrate into her bloodstream. She was glad she had taken care of it now. The longer you went, the more painful the process became for the dragon *and* the rider. At the stage it was at right now, it was only uncomfortable for Chine. After a drawn-out battle, it was like having salt thrown on a wound.

For Alex, the difference was in how much her blood heated. Either way, it was going to hurt, but absorbing this much hot fluid into her body was easily doable. After a couple of minutes, the heat in her veins disappeared. She decided to take a brief break to look at that tactical planner.

Alex opened her anchor and looked through its menus until she found the planner. She clicked it, and a virtual board opened in front of her. The board was mapped in a sixty-mile radius around her position.

There were figures representing Alex, Jim, and Chine, along with figures representing the descending ship, the mass of flying dark creatures, and the land monsters hunting the ship. "Whoa!" Alex exclaimed, "Now that is kinda cool."

Alex jumped off of the dragon and waved Jim over to her. "You gotta check this out," she told him. He wasted no time. "We have a pretty good look at the lay of the land from this thing right here."

Jim took a look at the hologram. "I think it's only showing what you've already seen. Look here. You don't have anything displayed over that hill. I think it's because we can't see over it."

A little of the excitement left Alex. She wished she had paid close enough attention to have seen that for herself. Still, she was glad Jim had brought it to her attention. "Okay, well, then I know what we're doing next. We need to map out the rest of this terrain."

Alex commed Jollies and asked, "So, where are those reinforcements?"

"I'm nearly there!" Jollies answered.

"Wait! I thought you said you were finding reinforcements?"

"Since you're so good at listening, you might remember me saying almost no one is here. We don't have enough bodies to leave their stations, but Brath said he'd take care of the night watch on his own until a replacement came by, so I flew out here to help you."

Alex would have preferred another couple dozen riders, but Jollies was more than competent on her dragon. Besides, if Alex was being honest, she would have taken Gill, Jollies, and even Brath over twenty other riders. "All right, Jollies. I got something for you when you get here."

"Kinda figured we weren't going to have time to wait for reinforcements. You know, since they're not coming."

Alex stared down at the blank spots of the hologram map. She was going to start acquainting herself with those invisible factors.

CHAPTER SEVEN

Gill and Jollies arrived at Alex's and Jim's coordinates around the same time. Jollies was riding Amber, an electric dragon proportionate to Jollies' small frame. The two were a good match, but it was always funny to see Jollies with the rest of the squad. Jollies was small enough to fit in Alex's palm, but she had a personality the size of a mountain.

Gill rode Timber, an earth dragon. He was a muted brown with relaxed scales and unassuming claws and fangs—a dragon perfectly suited for Gill, who was a quiet drow. Gill rarely raised his voice to anything above his usual deep, soft tone. It was hard to tell when he was excited. Unlike Jollies, his skin didn't change color with his mood.

The two dragonriders jumped off their dragons and came over to where Alex and Jim were sitting. Jim and Gill exchanged a quick hug, Gill asking Jim something Alex couldn't hear. Even if Gill wasn't so soft-spoken, Alex still probably wouldn't have been able to hear because Jollies came flying up to her ear, speaking rapidly.

Alex politely pulled Jollies away from her ear and placed the pixie on her shoulder. "Hold on, hold on. I'll tell you everything later. We have something more pressing to take care of."

Jollies flashed bright red and crossed her arms. "What makes you think I wasn't talking about the mission?"

"Were you asking me about the mission?"

Jollies didn't answer right away. Finally, she said, "No."

Alex pulled up the tactical display and nodded smugly. "That's what I thought you were going to say." Alex sighed. "Well, might as well get down to business. You guys know about the incoming ship. Hey, how come Brath didn't come?"

"We couldn't both leave. And yeah, we clocked the ship after you called us. It must still have power because it's descending so slowly. It's not a crash-landing."

Alex pointed to the tactical display, noting their position and the position of the ship. She drew their attention to the creatures that were in the valley and those above the ship. "Looks like we're not the only ones trying to pick this thing up, and if it's important to the Dark One, then it's important to us. I doubt if it's supplies or anything like that. From what I could see, the vrosks were trying to rip the thing to shreds in the air."

Gill leaned close to look at the display, his hair falling over his face. "This is a welcome addition to our tech," he said before straightening up and opening his display. "Formulating plans will be much easier. *If* you've decided to start planning things, that is?"

A few months ago, Alex would have gotten defensive, but she'd grown pretty familiar with Gill's wry sense of humor. That jab was as close to a joke as Gill ever got. "Yeah, I figured it might be the best route to keep from getting our heads blown off. And I'm open to contributions."

Gill smiled as he brushed his hair out of his face. "I'd like to hear what you're proposing first."

Alex pointed to the blank spots on the map display, east

of where they were currently. "The ship is heading in that direction and we don't know what's there. The descent is still pretty slow, so we can easily make it there before the ship does. I want Jollies to do a quick recon of the area and give us an idea of what we're walking into since she's the fastest."

Jollies zipped back over to her dragon and climbed aboard. "The display will automatically update for you guys?"

Alex nodded as she pointed to it. "That's what it did last time. I'm pretty sure it's sourcing information from our HUDs and dragon anchors."

"Okay, I'll be back ASAP. Don't do anything fun without me."

Jollies took off, heading east toward whatever lay over the hills.

Alex turned her attention to Gill. "I want you to check out the hills. You're the quietest of us all, and the only one I trust to get a better picture of what's trailing the ship. Jim's mech is too loud, and it's not a secret that I'm not good at laying low."

Gill nodded, turned off his display, and went back to his dragon. He left without saying a word, rising into the sky like a giant black cloud and disappearing.

Jim went back to his mech and jumped inside. "So, I'm guessing my role is to sit here quietly and do nothing?"

"Not nothing, but I don't have anything specific for you to do. Ideas?"

Jim looked at his tactical display. "No, I think you're right. I just don't like having to sit on the sidelines because of the whole mech thing, but like you said, the thing is too damn loud and not nearly as maneuverable as your dragons. Sneaking makes sense, and I can't do what Gill is about to."

Alex wondered if there was a hint of jealousy in Jim's voice. She could have just been hearing something that wasn't there. And then she wondered why she would hope Jim would be jealous of Gill. That didn't make any sense.

Jim was playing with the controls on his mech. "At least I can calibrate this thing," he muttered under his breath. "Got a feeling we're going to need heavy firepower in a little bit. I didn't need to get close to see there are a lot of monsters trying to get into that ship."

Alex had climbed back onto Chine and was scratching the dragon behind his horns. *What do you think is in the ship?*

Hopefully an enemy of the Dark One. We could always use more allies, Chine answered.

Wouldn't that be sweet?

At best, maybe it is something to help end this war sooner.

It took Jollies less than an hour to return, but the tactical display was updated long before that. Alex could appreciate why Myrddin had added it to their tools. As soon as Jollies had arrived at the valley and done the survey, the display had changed. If something had happened to Jollies, Lord forbid, it wouldn't have kept the team from receiving the intel.

Gill, on the other hand, took a little bit longer to get back. The three dragonriders were patiently waiting for him around a fire they had started. They watched the ship continue to descend. Alex was surprised the vrosks hadn't gotten inside yet. She'd seen what vrosks could do up close, and it wasn't pretty.

Jollies was already bored with waiting, and she'd only gotten back a few minutes ago. She paced up and down the length of a tree branch until finally jumping from the tree and landing on Alex's shoulder. "Okay, if you aren't going to give me any details now, the least you can do is tell me what you did," she whined.

Alex wanted to flick Jollies off her shoulder and let the conversation end there, but she knew it was because she was getting anxious, waiting for Gill to get back. Sending members of her team out alone always made her uncomfortable. "Fine," Alex relented. "We got into a fight with some giants and ended up running across a bunch of pixies living in the forest."

"Figures you two would get into a fight on a date. And there are pixies out here in the forest? I had no idea. What were they like?"

"Actually, now that I think of it, they were different from you or any of the pixies in the Nest. Not nearly as high energy. They were still beautiful, though."

"That's because the pixies in the Nest, including me, aren't woodland pixies. Most of us come from pixie cities. Things move faster there. Roy said it was like the difference between humans who grow up in the country or something called New York. Anyway, I'd like to meet them at some point. I haven't spent a whole lot of time with woodlanders."

"Is that a common thing? I mean, not knowing much about another branch of your own race?"

Jollies shrugged. "Depends on how you look at it. Most high elves don't know much about drow other than what they've read. I've heard it's the same for you humans. You don't know much about humans in other countries. Isn't that the basis for most of your wars?"

Alex couldn't disagree with her. "One of our leaders, a long time ago, said the only way humans would stop fighting each other was if we had to work together to fight something bigger than us."

Jollies laughed as Alex chuckled ironically. "That's a sad thought," the pixie whispered. "But I think you could say that about any of the races throughout the realms. Even the elves, regardless of what they'd have you think. Gnomes are the only race that has had an extended peace."

Alex found that hard to believe. "Really? Brath seems so angry, and so do all the other gnomes."

"That's just because gnomes are prickly. They haven't had a war in hundreds of years. That's why their homeworld fell so quickly. They had the weakest army of anyone attacked."

Alex let that irony sink in as she leaned forward and stared into the flames. She could see Jim's face through the fire, also pondering what Jollies had just said. He'd been quiet since the recalibrations on his mech had been finished—deep in thought, his eyes distant.

Behind Jim, Alex saw Gill's dragon land. The rider walked up to the flames and took a seat next to Jim, who patted him on the shoulder. "Glad you made it back," Jim said. "These two were trying their best to depress the living hell out of me."

Jollies stuck her tongue out at him. "I was not trying to depress you. We were just talking about the war."

Gill nodded as he scooted closer to the fire. "A good conversation for light hearts. It is something we should talk about. It makes no sense to fight a war we don't understand, even if it concerns us. Otherwise, we aren't much better than the Dark One's tools."

"Do drow have wars?" Alex asked.

Gill took his time answering, as he did anytime he was questioned about drow culture. At first, Alex had thought it was because he didn't want to talk to outsiders about his people. Over time, Alex had determined that it was more about trying not to misrepresent his people. "We drow haven't fought a war for some time. Maybe a few thousand years."

"How do you settle differences, then?"

"Most drow aggression is done through subterfuge.

Behind the scenes kind of stuff. The drow are technically at peace with everyone but really at peace with no one. It's one of the reasons people don't trust us. When your entire race is known for being sneaky, it's hard to get people to see anything other than that."

The four dragonriders sat in silence, watching the flames and thinking over what had been said. Then Alex pulled up her tactical display and announced, "We better start planning. Come on."

CHAPTER EIGHT

Alex discovered within minutes that she hated planning anything more than a few steps ahead, but she wanted to get better at it. Obviously, trusting her gut was only going to keep her out of trouble for so long. Planning ahead seemed like the best way to stay alive.

It also helped that she wasn't going at it by herself. The tactical display allowed everyone to see what was going on and chip in. That was great because both Gill and Jollies had excellent insights into some of the proposed ideas.

The four dragonriders sketched out an idea of how long it was going to take the ship to actually touch down. While they were charting the potential crash site of the ship, Alex received a comm from Myrddin. He told her he'd arrived back at Middang3ard and was in the process of pulling together whatever reinforcements he could. Obviously, his call for reinforcements held much more weight than Jollies' and Brath's.

After that was taken care of, Alex looked at the game plan the four had come up with. Gill and Jollies were going to try to clear out the area where the ship was going to land. From the recon the two had performed, it didn't seem like the Dark One's ground troops knew for sure where the ship was going. They seemed to be just guessing, and thanks to the combination of the tactical display, Alex's eyes, and Gill's and Jollies' recons, the dragonriders were fairly certain they had a better projection of where the ship was going.

If there were any of the Dark One's ground forces in the area, Jollies and Gill could get started taking care of them. If the ground forces were too numerous, they could radio for backup from Alex and Jim. There wasn't much distance between the two areas, and it would be easy enough to move back and forth as long as they weren't overrun.

Jim and Alex were going to try to thin the herd of monsters that were heading to the ship. If the giants suddenly decided to change course, there was going to be a much worse problem. It was better to take them out now instead of waiting until they posed a threat. That was where the valley and its surrounding hills were going to come in handy.

At the moment, Alex and Jim were outnumbered by the giants. The plan was to use the rocks and boulders on the hills to take out some of them, bringing the total down to a more manageable number.

The dragonriders went over their plan one more time, asking questions here and there when they needed clarification. It was straightforward enough, and the only thing that could really go wrong was incorrectly predicting where the ship was going to come down. Even if that happened, they could all easily correct their course once they had cleared out the Dark One's forces, though.

Alex flipped down her tactical display and stood. "You guys ready to get going?"

Jollies groaned as she floated on her back. "I wish I had known it was going to be a mission like this," she whined. "I would have brought along something to eat."

Jim went to his mech and pulled out a picnic basket. "Go crazy, you guys," he said as he tossed the basket to Alex. It was filled with sandwiches nicked from the cafeteria, along with a selection of desserts and treats. Alex noticed he had included some gnomish hard candy as well, one of Alex's favorites.

Gill picked around until he found some fruit. "I'm sorry you two won't be able to finish your picnic," he said softly. "The lake was probably beautiful at this time of day."

Alex reached over Gill's hand to grab a piece of jerky. "Yeah, it was. Jim told me you let him know about the place, right?"

Gill nodded, his face betraying no emotion, as usual. "When he told me you were going on a date, I could think of no better location," he replied. "Glad you enjoyed it. Jim, you and I are going to have to go swimming there soon. Brath still hasn't been either."

Jim grabbed a sandwich and started to scarf it down. "Sounds good to me. Honestly, after all this crap is finished, it might be nice to go for a dip before we head back to HQ. It's hot all night, right?"

"I didn't bring any swimming clothes."

Jim laughed as he took another bite of his sandwich. "I highly doubt anyone in our company is going to complain about seeing your ass. And it won't be anything I haven't seen."

Alex felt her face burning bright red and tried to find something to look at. Unfortunately, her eyes fell on Jollies, who was an even brighter red than Alex. Jim was having way too much fun with all this. "If you guys are done messing around, I'm ready to get going," Alex said.

Gill smiled politely as he took a seat underneath Timber's wings. "I'd prefer a little more time to eat if possible. Like Jollies, I haven't had a chance to eat."

Alex couldn't argue with him. Everyone else was still in the process of eating, even if she was starting to get anxious, waiting around. That, and it would be easier to avoid being teased if they were in active pursuit.

Alex walked over to the picnic basket and looked for something that looked appetizing. "You know, this is the first time we've all been around for a meal in a few weeks, I think."

Jim chewed as he nodded, scratching his chin. "Yeah, it has been a while. I can't remember the last time we all had lunch or dinner together."

"You would think things would have slowed down after the last mission. Seems like I hardly see you guys anymore unless we're trying to save the world or something."

Gill looked up from his food. "I don't think any of our missions have qualified as saving the realm yet, but I do understand the sentiment. I miss you guys as well. Brath does too, even if he'd prefer not to say it."

They were right. It had been a while since she and Jollies had spent any time with each other, even though they lived together. Today was the first day she'd seen Jim for longer than twenty minutes. Gill had been pretty much a shadow for the last two weeks. "We should make this happen more often. Minus the part where we have to chase a spaceship and kill a bunch of giants."

Jim finished his sandwich. "Yeah, I could do with more hanging out and fewer threats of death. That sounds like a much better way to spend my holiday."

Alex placed her hand in the middle of the group. "Promise. We all make sure to have a life outside of missions. And I'm going to count you as Brath, Gill."

Gill placed his hand on top of Alex's, and Jim placed his on top of Gill's. Jollies landed atop the pile of hands and nodded solemnly. "Promise."

Jim and Gill repeated the promise as well, then removed their hands. "Good. Now let's go save a spaceship."

CHAPTER NINE

Alex and Jim took off toward the rocky hills that rolled through the green valley as the ship above continued its slow, constant descent from the heavens. Alex couldn't keep herself from wondering what was inside. All of the time she'd spent with the riders had been concerned with how they were going to get to the ship, not its contents.

That could have been because none of them wanted to think about the last time they'd had to deal with anything from space. Their last excursion had ended up with them defying direct orders, most of them nearly dying, a harrowing psychedelic experience, possibly sharing a mind-meld with the Dark One, and Alex losing her arm.

It was easier not to talk about those things, and on the whole, that was what Team Boundless had been doing. That was probably why they hadn't been seeing much of each other. Sitting in a room with Jollies for too long would have prompted conversations Alex didn't want to have. She was already getting weird looks from other students. Everyone's eyes gravitated toward her arm.

Alex hadn't had a chance to have the robotic nature of her arm covered. Myrddin had mentioned something about it when it was first installed, and now she almost wished she had gone the magical route instead. She still wasn't used to seeing steel bones instead of skin, but then again, she was only recently getting used to seeing anything.

The arm worked perfectly and she rarely realized it wasn't the one she'd been born with, except when she accidentally exerted too much strength. But she was quickly learning to control that.

Alex had been glad to be alone with Jim for a little bit but had been worried the conversation was going to turn to her arm, or even worse, what she'd seen within the meteor that had fallen from the sky.

The experience had been too much to wrap her head around. Sometimes she would think about it during the day, and a well of dread would creep into her stomach, the room would get distant, and things would become fuzzy. She tried to keep from thinking about it.

That didn't stop the nightmares, though. Alex had never been so happy Jollies was a night person as when they had returned from that mission. The nightmares had arrived in droves, each of them concerned with the rock in some way. She hardly remembered them when she woke. She figured it was just stress, but part of her worried there might be something deeper. She had been connected to the Dark One or one of his minions on a mental plane. Maybe she'd brought something back with her.

Alex shook her head. That was why she had been avoiding everyone, even her own thoughts. Studying was easier. Hell, getting lost in a crush was easier too.

As Alex looked at the green streak left by the ship, she couldn't push aside the fear growing in the back of her throat like a bad nasal drip. Soon her hands were going to start shaking, then she was going to throw up. After that, she'd be useless.

Alex wondered where all this fear had just come from. Only a couple of seconds ago, there had been nothing. She'd been fine. Maybe meeting with the Nest's shrink wasn't such a bad idea. Talking almost sounded nice. Alex wished she could have talked this over with her parents, but they would have worried. But if they could get past the worry, they would have understood.

The hills were coming up. *Time to get your head in this,* Alex thought as she focused on the giants who were riding mammoths across the plains. Alex wouldn't have assumed mammoths could move so fast, but those things were hauling ass. Hopefully, they'd be able to make it to the boulders before the mammoths passed.

Chine's mind tugged at hers. Sometimes when there had been a long interval, Chine would politely nudge Alex before interrupting her thoughts. *What's up, Chine?*

The dragon's thoughts were soft and almost timid. As the two got closer, Alex was starting to pick up on the emotions behind his words. *You seem distracted, Dustling. As if something is troubling you.*

Alex should have known better than to not talk to Chine about it. She should have at least let him know what was going through her mind. Even if she tried to hide her feelings from him, he usually picked something up, and they needed to be in sync. They depended too much on each other.

This is too much like last time, Alex finally said. *It's freaking me out. The last time, it was...*

I know, Chine replied. *I was there. I'd never felt anything like that before. It was disturbing.*

What if this is the same thing?

Alex felt her dragon's positivity wash over her and wrap around her like a warm blanket. It was almost as good as getting a hug from her dad. *It isn't going to be the same. For one thing, if this were nearly as dangerous as the rock was, Myrddin would have had it on his map for months. And whatever it turns out to be, we'll be able to handle it.*

He was right. If this thing was as dangerous as the meteor, there was no way Myrddin wouldn't have prepared for this situation. That was all the wizard did. And, Alex reminded herself, reinforcements were on the way. Maybe this would be an easy one.

Except for the horde of giants riding mammoths. Comparatively, though, that wasn't as bad.

Alex and Jim sped up, flying around the giants so as not to give away their position until they got to the hills. They found a spot with a number of boulders. Alex pulled up her tactical display to see how Jollies and Gill were doing.

The display showed that the other two dragonriders weren't too far from their destination. Alex commed Jollies and asked, "What's it look like out there?"

Jollies' voice came back instantly, a little garbled. "We got A LOT of bogies. That's what you call 'em, right? Or tangos? I don't know. I'm not sure I've been getting all the targeting slang. Whatever. Wargs and orcs. Same ol', same ol'. Tons of 'em."

"What's the game plan?"

"Uh, Gill, what are you thinking? Short and sweet?"

Gill spoke over the comm. "I believe I could sneak around to the front and draw most of their attention as you split them down the middle."

"Oh, like that two-point pattern you were showing me?"

"Exactly."

Alex was impressed by the obvious teamwork between

the two. She was a little jealous but wasn't sure of who. Either way, it was good they knew what they were going to be doing. "All right, sounds great. Let me know if anything changes, okay?"

"No probs. Jollies out."

Jim was already in position to get the boulders going. Alex got behind him. Once the first two went down, they were going to have to rush over to the next couple and keep going. The only way this was going to work was if they got the jump on the giants. Taking too long between rolling the boulders would let the giants catch their breath and maybe mount an attack.

After they depleted the hills of boulders, the only other option was to get up close and personal with their targets. These didn't seem to be yhomir. They were much larger. Alex reminded herself that close didn't mean too close.

Alex looked at Jim and gave him the high sign. Chine reared up on his hind legs and slammed his chest into the boulder as Jim fired a concussive blast at the boulder in front of him.

Both Jim's and Alex's boulders started to roll down the ridge. Neither of the riders wasted any time jumping over to the next boulder and pushing it. Then on to the next. And the next after that.

Alex worked as fast as she could, and it wasn't long until they had cleared the first hill of all the boulders. She pulled up on her dragon anchor, sending Chine bolting for the ridge across from her as Jim's mech rose. She landed and started the process again with the boulders on the other side.

The boulders Alex and Jim had already gotten moving were picking up speed as they careened down the slopes into the mostly flat valley.

Alex took off and held out her anchor, pulling her scythe

out of the ether. "Let's get this done," she said before taking off toward the giants.

Chine dipped into the valley as the boulders Alex and Jim had set loose slammed into the mammoth's body, knocking the creature to its knees and tossing the giant from its back.

As Chine got closer, Alex could see just how massive the creatures were. These giants were nearly twenty feet tall. They were large enough to swat at Alex and Chine if they got too close. That put an end to one of Alex's plans. She had originally planned on raining fire from above. Now that she could see how large the giants were, it became obvious that to do any real damage, she was going to have to be close enough that she would be in range of the giants.

Jim seemed to realize the same thing because he pulled up to give himself time to figure out what to do.

The boulders were still crashing into the giants. Luckily, the boulders were large enough to do damage. They were knocking over the giants and mammoths left and right. It was difficult to see if the giants were going to stay down, but some of the boulders were roughly the size of a giant and a mammoth together.

Alex was glad they had put time into coming up with a plan. If they had just walked blindly into this fight, they would not have survived.

As Alex and Jim continued to gauge what was going on below them, one of the giants who had been knocked over got to his feet. He grabbed bits of the boulder that had exploded against his mammoth's legs and began throwing them at the riders.

Chine dodged the rock, but Jim took a direct hit to his shoulder-mounted machine gun. He threw on his thrusters, putting more distance between him and the giants. If that was how fast they could throw shrapnel, Jim was going to need more space to maneuver. The mech wasn't as fast as Chine.

Alex worried for a second that all they had managed to do was provide ammo for the giants, but it seemed like most of the ones who had been knocked over were also knocked out. There were only half as many as there had been before.

One of the giants, the one who had thrown the boulder shards, had a gnarled face, its nose looking like it had been carved from a tree, its eyes deep and heavy, with sadness buried within them. He reached down to his side and pulled out a long, curved horn made from a mammoth tusk. He blew into it, releasing a mournful call that echoed through the valley.

Alex sighed loudly as she shouted to Jim, "Whatever the hell that is, it's not going to be good!"

As Alex shouted, the giant beneath her blew his horn again. "Not going to have any more of that," Alex said as she drew her plasma pistol. She took aim and fired, and the horn shattered.

The giant below her smiled, its teeth dark and stained. Then it pulled a black rod from his side and aimed it at Alex. The giant shouted something and Alex felt a wave of energy wash over her, pushing her back. The force of the energy got stronger, shoving Chine back as well.

As Chine tilted backward, Alex felt her feet lifting off Chine's back. They were no longer anchored. She frantically grabbed her dragon anchor, which was flickering on and off. "Oh, crap, oh crap!" Alex shouted as she floundered, trying to grab something to hang onto.

Alex wasn't fast enough. She knew the fall was going to hurt, but she needed to think fast. If she wasn't anchored to Chine, that meant the giants had something that would sever their connection. If they could do it once, they could do it again. Alex was going to be fending for herself.

As the dragon anchor flickered, Alex whipped her hand out again and pulled her scythe out right before the anchor cut off. She clutched the hilt tightly as the giants ahead of her watched her fall. "There really aren't *any* easy missions," she muttered.

CHAPTER TEN

On the ground, Alex felt powerless. Even with her scythe in her hand, without Chine, she felt like she was simply waiting to die. Fear had overcome her faster than any emotion ever had. Dozens of eyes glared at her from what was quickly becoming a haze, those of the giant who had pulled her from Chine's back burning brightest of them all.

Alex looked upward, trying to find Chine. It looked like vrosks had detached from the ship above and were now attacking the dragon, trying to keep him away from Alex.

Whoever had organized this attack had figured out a vital aspect of the dragonriders. Dragon was the first part of the job title, rider came second.

Alex glanced at her anchor. It still wasn't up and running. She wasn't sure if that meant her connection to Chine was broken or not. As far as Alex knew, their connection was mental and based in Chine's biology, not the tech attached to Alex's arm. *Chine, can you hear me?* she called.

Chine's voice boomed in Alex's head. *Yes, Alex, I am still here. Are you okay?*

The giants were beginning to advance, the one carrying the black rod ahead of the rest, his club resting on his shoulder.

Alex took a step back, her scythe trembling in her hand. *Uh, I am for the moment. But I'm staring at a bunch of giants. Get your ass back down here, please. As fast as you can.*

Chine groaned in pain, and Alex looked up in time to see Chine whirling, trying to get away from the vrosks that were swarming him. *Chine!* Alex called.

Chine let loose a jet of fire, but he was still being overwhelmed. *I can't get away,* Chine shouted. *They must have been planning on separating us. You will have to fight alone until I can get back to you, Alex. Fight well.*

Alex's legs buckled as she took another step back, scanning the air for Jim. She hit her comm but heard nothing. The comms were connected to the dragon anchor. She was alone.

The ground thundered as the group of giants took another step toward Alex. *Oh my God oh my God oh my God,* Alex thought, the words reverberating in her skull. *What am I going to do?*

The scythe wasn't large enough. She was too small and not nearly strong enough. There were too many giants and mammoths. What the hell was a dragonrider without a dragon? If this were *Middang3ard* VR, this would have been an instant game over, but it wasn't. Here it meant a slow, agonizing death.

The giant with the black rod stepped away from the rest of the giants as thunder cracked above and rain began to pour. "Ah, you are the human we were warned about," the giant boomed, his voice nearly as loud as the thunder. "What do they call you?"

Alex's voice stuck in her throat. She knew she was being

taunted but couldn't answer, simply standing in silence as the giant gloated at her fear.

The leader of the giants pounded his chest and shouted, "Are you a mute as well as a cripple?" He pointed at Alex's robotic hand. "Let me inform you of the name of the one who will bring your death. I am Hulmor, the First Giant of the Dark One. I will grind your bones up after I tear away your flesh."

Alex knew she should run, but there was nowhere to go. The giants were much larger than her. She'd be caught in a matter of seconds. Where the hell was Jim? What was he doing up there?

Maybe I can stall until Chine can get down here, Alex thought. "How are you going to do that from all the way over there?" she shouted.

"Oh, so the mouse can speak?" Hulmor chuckled. "After we break you, I'll boil you alive. That way, you will come right apart, and your bones will crack easier."

"Break me? Are you talking emotionally or physically? You're gonna have to be more specific because, I mean, I think I might be emotionally broken already. The last few months have been a hell storm. I saw a bunch of kids at my school die. Then my mind got flayed by your boss and his weird son/child thing or whatever. Oh, and I got dragged into a cross-dimensional rescue mission."

Alex didn't know why all those words were pouring out of her, but once she started, she couldn't stop. They just kept flowing. "I mean, I have a crush on two guys. Which is, like, the least of all my problems. But I really wish it was just my only problem. I miss my parents, and I'm worried how upset and terrified they'd be if they found out how dangerous my life is."

The giants looked at each other, obviously confused by

the rant Alex was giving. Even Hulmor looked puzzled by how the situation was playing out.

Alex started pacing, rubbing her temple with her free hand. "I mean, I am *exhausted*. Like, *really* exhausted. I've never been this tired in my whole life, and I don't feel like I can get anything right. I mean, it's not like I'm doing anything wrong. It just feels like it's not right. Not good enough. Even this! Chine's fighting his ass off up there, and I'm sitting here freaking out about whether I'm going to get killed or not. *He* could get killed. Jim could already be dead! I mean—"

Hulmor clapped his hands, interrupting Alex by shouting, "Human, I think you are confused by—"

"I am NOT FINISHED!" Alex shrieked, the air around her instantly growing hot, a concussive wave of energy streaming out of her body as her eyes flashed red. And just like that, the energy was gone. "But I guess if you want to get all fight-y, let's get this done. Is it really going to take a dozen of you to kill one human?"

Hulmor still looked stunned by the variety of moods Alex had just gone through. He quickly composed himself, though, and laughed cruelly. "It won't take any more than me to—"

Jim's mech crashed into the group of giants, his machine gun firing as he launched two missiles that sent a giant and mammoth flying. Then he leaped among the flurry of flames and bullets lighting the air.

Above, she heard the roaring of mechs as their thrusters cut through the silence of the night. Some of them were heading toward the ship in the distance, and the rest were getting ready to land in the valley with Alex and the giants. "Guess you don't have a choice," Alex shouted. "Looks like your friends are gonna have enough on their hands."

Alex had no idea why she was goading the giant. Chine

was still nowhere to be seen, and her dragon anchor still wasn't online. The brief moment of confidence that had flared up was gone, and she was reminded that she was a very small human standing up to a very large giant.

The giant didn't need a reminder. He leaped through the air, his club high. Alex lunged to the side, rolling away as the club hit the ground where she had stood, tearing up the earth. Even though the giant was huge, he was fast.

Alex scrambled away from the giant as he chased her, swinging his club. As the club arced down, Alex turned to see it was going to smash into her face. She pulled up her scythe, narrowly blocking the club. The force of the attack sent her skidding back, but she was still on her feet.

Alex looked down at her robotic arm. Steam was coming off of it as its cylinders reset. Alex knew she was stronger on any realm except Earth, but the attack from the giant would have knocked her out a few weeks ago. Maybe the robotic arm wasn't such a bad idea.

As was usually the case now, Alex switched her scythe to her robotic arm and twirled it once to get used to the weight. *Maybe I can do this,* she thought. *I fought giants earlier today. I'm just fighting another giant now. A larger one, that's all.*

Alex dashed forward as fast as she could, then leaped, spinning in a quarter circle as she slashed at the giant.

Hulmor raised his club, absorbing the force of the blow. It didn't seem to have fazed him. Alex didn't care. She'd seen the difference between herself and the giant, one Alex rarely noticed because she was always with Chine.

Alex was ridiculously fast.

Alex, still in the air, whipped around, twirling her scythe behind her back, and slashed again at Hulmor, who had to take a step back before she attacked again. Her next few attacks were relentless, her robotic arm steaming with each attack.

Hulmor continued to back up, barely able to move his club in time to catch her blows.

Alex hit the ground and caught her breath, sizing up the situation. She didn't want to just run into this. She'd done that enough. Alex wanted to understand the fight. That didn't mean she couldn't trust her gut. It just meant there was more to her than that.

There had been a flash of something earlier. Alex had felt it. Fiery energy had given her a boost of confidence. Could it have been the augment she and Chine shared, the one that allowed her to make use of the draconic fluid in her dragon anchor? How had she accessed it before?

The last thing Alex had remembered before the sudden surge of energy was getting angry at being cut off. Maybe it was anger that triggered it.

Alex tried to think of something that pissed her off. Surprisingly, it wasn't difficult, but nothing happened.

Hulmor was breathing heavily but unwilling to betray his weariness. "Do you need a break, human?" he taunted.

Alex looked around the battlefield. The mechs above were helping Chine take care of the vrosks on his back. Jim and the other mechs were cutting down the rest of the giants and mammoths. Now that Alex thought about it, this mission hadn't been hard. "No," Alex called. "Let's finish this."

Hulmor and Alex ran toward each other. The giant went for the attack and Alex pushed herself a little harder, felt her legs aching as she tried for extra speed. Then, there it was—that flash again. She felt flames burst out over her body for a second as she gained a massive speed boost.

Alex slid under her opponent's legs, stretched out her scythe, and slashed as she turned in a circle. The giant let out a scream of pain as his legs separated from his feet at the ankles.

Hulmor hit the ground, screaming in pain as his stumps

bled. Alex looked down at the giant, reeling from the sickening gore.

Alex forced herself to remember what she was doing. Why she was here. That she was at war. She swallowed hard, reminding herself that Hulmor would have torn her to shreds if he had gotten the chance.

The scythe was raised and it fell, putting an end to Hulmor's pained mutters of revenge.

Alex looked down at her dragon anchor as it turned back on. Then she went over to Hulmor's body and picked up the black rod he had used to disconnect her from the Chine. She pocketed it before reaching out to her dragon. *Hey, buddy, you still okay?*

Chine landed right behind Alex, causing her to jump in surprise. *A simple yes would have been enough,* she said as she leaped onto his back.

As the dragon took off, he said, *I saw your fight. You didn't need my assistance. Perhaps you needed me to stay out of it,* he said.

The rest of the skirmish was clearing out. The mechs had made short work of the giants and mammoths. *Yeah, maybe I did need that,* Alex said. *It's different when you aren't there. Kinda terrible, you know? It's easy to forget what I'm doing when everything is moving so fast, or you're just chomping and burning through everything. Maybe I need to remember.*

Chine didn't answer, so Alex was left to interpret his silence. Instead of dwelling on it, she commed Jollies. "How did everything turn out on your end?"

Jollies sounded relaxed when she replied, "Easy-peasy."

"Good to hear. We're heading to the projected crash site right now."

Alex and the rest of the Team Boundless arrived at the landing site. The ship had descended much faster once the vrosks had been removed from its sides.

The relief was instant when Alex could see this was indeed a ship and nothing like the meteor she'd seen before. The ship could hardly be called that; if anything, it seemed like an escape pod. It was no larger than twenty feet in diameter and was a perfect sphere, only the outline of a potential door disturbing its smooth and polished surface.

Most of the mech riders were standing around, watching the ship. No one made a move. That was when Alex realized Team Boundless probably held rank in the situation. If Roy or the teachers weren't present, Boundless had the highest-ranking riders.

Alex looked at the rest of the team. "You guys want to come with me? I don't feel qualified to be an alien's first and only interaction. Plus, it'll let whoever it is know that this isn't one of those humans-are-the-best-and-rule-the-world kinda things."

Jollies flew over and landed on Alex's shoulder. "That's an odd human thing to say, but sure."

Jim and Gill came over to Alex as well, and they approached the scorched earth where the ship had landed.

Alex stood before it for some time with the rest of Boundless, but nothing seemed to be happening. She wasn't sure if the passenger had been hurt or if there was some kind of technical issue, but waiting seemed just as rude as ignoring it. Not knowing what else to do, Alex leaned forward and knocked twice on the door.

The ship shot steam out of several holes that appeared. The faint lines gradually became more pronounced until a door popped open.

As the steam dissipated, Alex could make out the shape

and features of whatever was inside the ship. It was humanoid and had a round head slightly larger than the rest of its body, the top of its head looking like a jewel of some sort. The creature had similar jeweled pieces on its chest, elbows, and knees.

The alien was oddly muscular, as if it were a fighter and regularly indulged in intense physical training. Its long, thick tail was curled around its waist. It was lying on the deck of the ship just inside the door.

Jim whistled as he took a step back. "That is not what I was expecting," he muttered before turning to Jollies and Gill. "You guys ever seen anything like that before?"

Gill shook his head as he watched the alien closely. "No," he finally replied. "I do not think this is from any of the known planets of the nine realms. This being is an alien to us all."

The alien's eyes fluttered open slowly. It began sitting up, groaning as it held its side. "Is this Middang3ard," the alien muttered in a faint, almost echoey voice.

Alex stepped forward and said, "Yes, this is Middang3ard. My name is Alex. This is Team Boundless. We're here to help you."

The alien nodded as it tried to sit up taller. "Good. Take me to whoever is in charge. I have a way to stop the Dark One once and for all."

Alex and the rest of Team Boundless exchanged glances as the mech riders murmured amongst themselves. "Hold on a second," she said as she took a step away and commed Myrddin.

Myrddin sounded as if he had sobered up considerably when he picked up. "Alex, how did the extraction go?"

"We found…an alien. He wants to meet with you. You're the one who's in charge of everything, right? Like, across the board."

"You could say that. A unit is already on its way. It should be there shortly."

As Myrddin hung up, the ground brightened with beams of light from an extraction vessel. The vessel floated in the sky like a hanging city block.

The alien in the escape pod covered its eyes as it stared up at the vessel. Alex came over, shielding her eyes as well. "Guess our ride is here. Welcome to Middang3ard." She extended her hand to the alien.

The alien looked at Alex's hand for a long time before understanding bloomed on its face. With a nod, it took the hand and, looking Alex in the eyes, said, "Thank you. I only hope I have arrived in time."

Alex was just exposed to an alien who has come here for mysterious reasons. Reasons that just might end the war with the Dark One. Find out what those reasons are in *An Alien Affair*.

AUTHOR NOTES RAMY VANCE

APRIL 3, 2020

I've been hard at work on follow-up last year's hit series – The Toddler.

Seems the Toddler is about to face his greatest challenge yet when a new heroes comes onto the scene.

Meet ... The Sibling ... Pray her nappy is dry.

Tired of the same old urban fantasy plot lines? Looking for something brand new and mind-bending?

Check out Ramy Vance's brand new series Urban Fantasy series: The Silbling

Last year, the Toddler saved the city from a powerful magic. After battling dragons and dirty diapers, the Toddler thought he was prepared to face anything.

But now that there's a new hero in town, the Toddler must face his greatest challenge yet. He must learn to share.

If you like the Dresden Files, Buffy the Vampire Slayer or Seasame Street, then you'll be helplessly addicted to The Toddler's spin-off series: The Sibling

COMING SOON!

Praise for The Sibling:

★★★★★ "Finally a breath of … well … seriously stinky air."

★★★★★ "Buffy meets Dora the Explorer."

★ ★ ★ ★ ★ "Move over Paw Patrol … Adventure Bay finally has a couple of real hero in town."

Can't wait? Don't worry, we got you covered. Check out Ramy Vance's Mortality Bites series.

Katrina Darling is an ex-vampire just trying to figure out how to be human again. Too bad her past has other ideas.

Critics are calling this series:

★ ★ ★ "Not nearly as good, but at least Kat is potty trained."

★ ★ "Why are you wasting our time with ex-vampires, kick-ass heroines and totally unique, magical settings. We want The Sibling!.. Bah, I guess this tripe is better than nothing."

Check out Mortality Bites today!

Click Here: readerlinks.com/l/767060

OTHER BOOKS BY THE AUTHORS

Other Middang3ard Books

Never Split The Party (01)
Late To the Party (02)
It's My Party (03)
Blue Hell And Alien Fire (04)

Death Of An Author: A Middang3ard Novella

Other Books by Ramy Vance

Mortality Bites Series
Keep Evolving Series
Fatebound Series
Welcome to the Dragon Show Series

Other Books by Michael Anderle

For a complete list of books by Michael Anderle, please visit:

www.lmbpn.com/ma-books/

All LMBPN Audiobooks are Available at Audible.com and iTunes. To see all LMBPN audiobooks, including those written by Michael Anderle please visit:

www.lmbpn.com/audible

CONNECT WITH THE AUTHORS

Connect with Ramy

Join Ramy's Newsletter

Join Ramy's FB Group: House of the GoneGod Damned!

Connect with Michael Anderle and sign up for his email list here:

Website: http://lmbpn.com

Email List: http://lmbpn.com/email/

Facebook:
www.facebook.com/TheKurtherianGambitBooks

www.ingramcontent.com/pod-product-compliance
Lightning Source LLC
Chambersburg PA
CBHW050158110726
47898CB00008B/2847